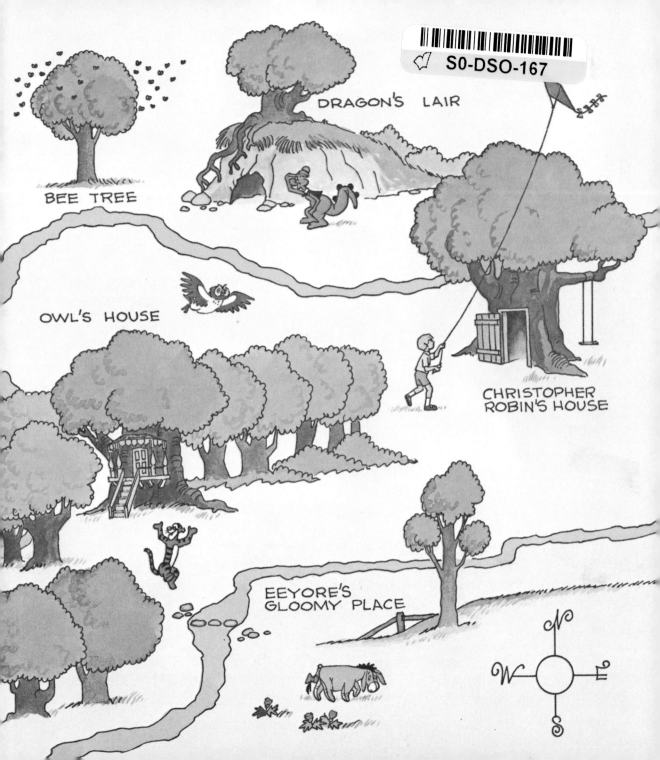

DRAGON'S LAIR

BEE TREE

OWL'S HOUSE

CHRISTOPHER
ROBIN'S HOUSE

EEYORE'S
GLOOMY PLACE

Exploring the
Hundred Acre Wood

Walt Disney

Productions'

Exploring the Hundred Acre Wood

Golden Press • New York

Western Publishing Company, Inc.

Racine, Wisconsin

Printed in the U.S.A. by Western Publishing Company, Inc.
GOLDEN® and GOLDEN PRESS® are trademarks of Western Publishing Company, Inc.
Library of Congress Catalog Card Number: 80-51162
ISBN 0-307-23206-9

EARLY one fine summer morning, Piglet appeared in Pooh's doorway. He looked unhappy.

"What's the matter?" asked Pooh sympathetically, since he was a very sympathetic bear.

"It's such a beautiful day," said Piglet, "and already I've wasted over an hour of it. I can't think of a thing to do. Absolutely not one thing."

"Nonsense," said Pooh, "there's always something to do."

"Like what?" asked Piglet.

"Like . . . uh . . . like . . ." Pooh's voice trailed off.

Piglet waited.

"I think we'd better see Christopher Robin," Pooh said finally. "He's very good at thinking of things."

Pooh and Piglet reached Christopher Robin's house just as he came outside. "It's a beautiful day," said Christopher Robin.

"Exactly," said Pooh, "and that's why we're here. We can't decide what to do with such a beautiful day."

"Oh!" said Christopher Robin. "Well, let's see who can think of something first."

They all sat down and thought. Finally Christopher Robin said, "Let's explore. Let's take a nature walk."

"Just what I was going to suggest," said Pooh.

"What's a nature walk?" asked Piglet.

"Well, Piglet," Christopher Robin said, "you walk quietly and look for interesting things like flowers and birds."

"And bees and honey trees," added Pooh.

Winnie-the-Pooh suggests some things you may want to take on a nature walk:

A box or a bag for collecting things

A thermos or canteen of water

A magnifying glass for looking at tiny things

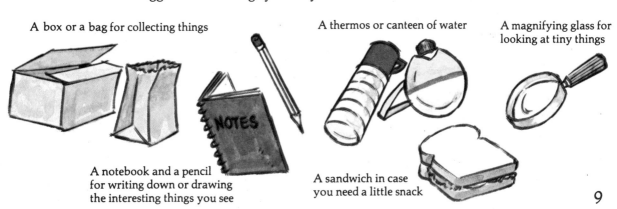

A notebook and a pencil for writing down or drawing the interesting things you see

A sandwich in case you need a little snack

9

Christopher Robin packed three slices of honey cake for Pooh and peanut butter and jelly sandwiches for Piglet and himself. He took along a book, too. "It's called BOOK OF INTERESTING THINGS TO KNOW," he said.

Then they set forth down a path in the Hundred Acre Wood. Pooh and Piglet were each carrying a bag for collecting interesting things. "I wonder who will be the first to find something interesting," Pooh remarked.

Here are some leaf pictures from Christopher Robin's book. Do you see the leaf that Piglet found?

beech leaf   sweetgum leaf   oak leaf

It was Piglet. "Look," he said, stooping to pick up something in the path. "A green star."

"Silly Piglet," said Christopher Robin. "That's a star-shaped leaf."

apple leaf

willow leaf

11

Pooh and Piglet decided to see which one of them could find more different kinds of leaves. They were scurrying about putting leaves in their sacks when Rabbit came hopping along. He was looking for one of his friends-and-relations.

"I think Very Small Beetle must be lost," Rabbit said. "I haven't seen him in days."

Here are three beetles from Christopher Robin's book:

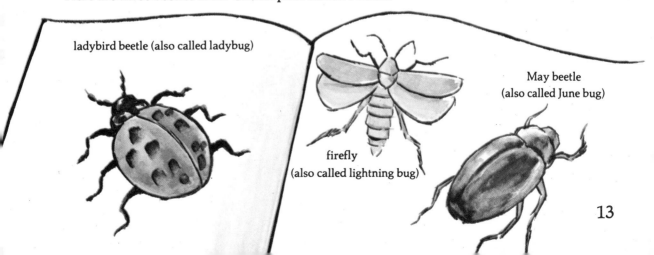

ladybird beetle (also called ladybug)

firefly
(also called lightning bug)

May beetle
(also called June bug)

"Well," said Christopher Robin, "we can be looking for Very Small Beetle while we're taking our nature walk."

After a while they came to the foot of the tallest oak tree in the Hundred Acre Wood. Pooh knew it well. Bees had found a hollow place in the tree and started a honey store in it.

"Let's think about bees and honey," Pooh said.

Rabbit hopped off to a near-by clover patch in search of Very Small Beetle. Christopher Robin, Pooh, and Piglet sat under a tree and talked about bees.

From Christopher Robin's book, here is a picture of a honeybee and some favorite flowers of the bees. Bees make their honey from the sweet nectar of these flowers. Umm-umm!

wild rose

clover

honeysuckle

15

"Well, I didn't find Very Small Beetle in the clover patch," announced Rabbit, "but I found a four-leaf clover!"

"And we didn't get any honey from the honey tree," complained Pooh. "The bees are very buzzy today."

"But I found five different leaves," said Piglet as they moved on.

Pooh was worried. He had been thinking about honey instead of leaves. Piglet's sack was beginning to look as though he might win the contest.

They came to a place where the grass was just right for sitting, so Pooh sat on it. Piglet sat down, too, on a rock. Suddenly the rock began to walk away with Piglet.

"Oh, help!" cried Piglet, "a walking rock."

"That's not a rock, Piglet," said Christopher Robin. "That's a turtle. And now you've frightened it. Look! It's pulled its head and legs inside its shell."

Warning from Christopher Robin for nature walkers: Go quietly. Step softly. Wild creatures are easily frightened. You'll see more of them if you take it slow and easy and watch.

"May I take the turtle home with me?" asked Piglet. "It has such a pretty shell."

"Better not," said Christopher Robin. "That turtle will be much happier right here where it belongs, near the water and near Rabbit's garden."

"Just so it doesn't eat my carrots or cabbages," Rabbit said, looking worried.

Interesting things to know about turtles from Christopher Robin's book:

Turtles eat fruit, particularly berries. (They might nibble on Rabbit's cabbage leaves or carrot tops, but not much.)

A turtle has no teeth, but the edges of its jaws are as sharp as a bird's beak. Here is a picture of the turtle that Piglet thought was a walking rock. It is called a painted turtle.

They came to the top of a grassy hill and decided to rest. Pooh leaned back and looked up at the blue sky. There were some nice, puffy clouds drifting above the Hundred Acre Wood.

"I can see one that makes me think of a honey pot," said Pooh. He sighed. "So many things make me think about honey pots. Perhaps that's why I'm a bear of some stoutness!"

Piglet began to laugh. "There's a cloud that looks like you, Rabbit. See, there's your tail and there are your ears."

But Rabbit was too busy searching for Very Small Beetle to look up.

Now the sun was high overhead and Christopher Robin decided that it was time to have lunch.

Pooh agreed. "This really looks like a picnic sort of place," he said.

They put their food on a tablecloth that Christopher Robin had brought along in his knapsack. Rabbit added a bouquet of fresh clover that he had picked for nibbling.

Suddenly Pooh felt a tickle on his foot and Piglet felt a prickle on his back. "Ants!" Pooh said.

"Why do they always come to picnics?" Piglet asked. "Does it say anything in your book about ants, Christopher Robin?"

About Ants, from Christopher Robin's book:

Ants live all over the world, so anyplace you have a picnic ants are nearby.

Ants love to eat sweet things. (So does Pooh!)

Ants have two stomachs. (Sometimes Pooh wishes he did, too.)

23

After the four nature walkers had finished eating, they carefully cleaned up their picnic place. Then they hiked to the bottom of the hill and crossed the stream to Eeyore's Gloomy Place. They asked Eeyore to join them.

Eeyore looked up at the bright blue sky. "Of course, it will probably rain," he said.

"Nonsense," said Rabbit. "We need another pair of good eyes to look for Very Small Beetle. Please come."

This rather pleased Eeyore. "There are other things to look for on a nature walk," he said solemnly as he walked along with them.

Eeyore says: Be careful what you touch in the woods. Some plants can give you an itchy rash. Stay away from these three:

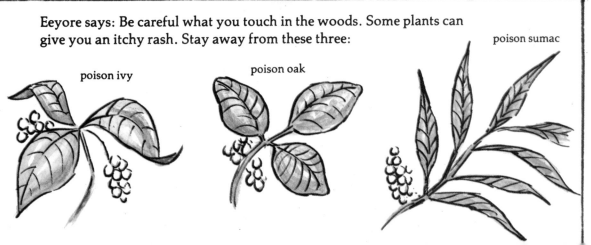

poison ivy

poison oak

poison sumac

They walked along, looking at all the interesting things on the ground and in the air. There were flowers and ferns, birds and butterflies, big rocks to sit on and little pebbles to throw in the stream, and many places to look for Very Small Beetle.

Suddenly Pooh blinked. A butterfly had fluttered up from a buttercup. "What frightened him?" Pooh asked.

Piglet wants you to see some of the things they saw in the meadow:

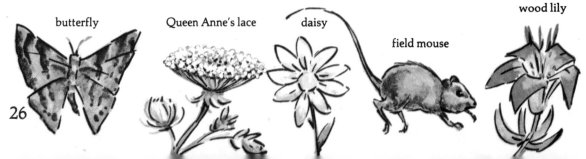

butterfly   Queen Anne's lace   daisy   field mouse   wood lily

"Me," said a jouncy sort of voice. Tigger came bounding out of the meadow.

"Oh, Tigger," Christopher Robin said. "Won't you join us on our nature walk?"

"I'm not a good nature walker," said Tigger. "I'm too springy." And he bounced away from them across the meadow.

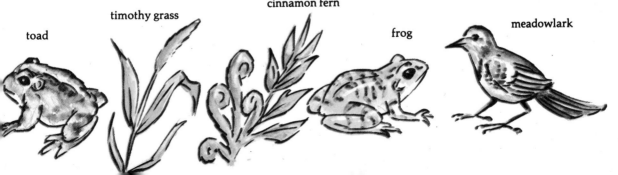

toad

timothy grass

cinnamon fern

frog

meadowlark

While Rabbit and Eeyore continued to search for
Very Small Beetle, Pooh and Piglet looked for interesting things to add to their collections. Piglet
found some pretty pebbles on the bottom of the stream.
Pooh picked up some brightly colored bird feathers.

In his BOOK OF INTERESTING THINGS TO KNOW,
Christopher Robin found a picture of each bird that
had lost a feather.

Here are the feathers that Pooh found.
Can you tell which feather came from which bird?

blue jay

redbird

blackbird

oriole

yellow warbler

brown thrasher

Rabbit looked under logs and by tree stumps and around ferns and wildflowers. "Hello, there," he called. "Are you there, Very Small Beetle?"

"Searching, searching," said Eeyore. "I bet if I were lost no one would look this hard for me." He shook his head. "But then why should they?"

There was no answer.

At last Christopher Robin suggested that since they were very near Owl's tree maybe he could help them. "Owls are very wise, you know," he said.

Owl heard them coming. He even heard what Christopher Robin said about him. "How true," he muttered to himself.

Owl wants everyone to know that:
Owls see very well. Although they see
best at night, they can also see in the daytime.
Owls are very good listeners, and when they
fly, they make scarcely a sound.

Owl decided that the searchers should divide into two groups and take different paths. In this way they would cover more ground and stand a better chance of finding Very Small Beetle.

So, Christopher Robin, Rabbit, and Owl set off towards Kanga's house. Eeyore, Pooh, and Piglet took the path that led to a bee tree. (Pooh suggested this.)

A little way along the path, Piglet saw some interesting animal tracks. "Oh, Pooh," he said, "I wonder what animal made those tracks?"

"Let's follow them and see," said Pooh, and they left the path. Eeyore, nose to the ground, didn't even see them go.

Pooh and Piglet followed the tracks into a thicket. In no time at all, they discovered that they were lost.

Here are some animal tracks. Which ones do you think Pooh and Piglet followed?

squirrel

Tigger

deer

fox

"Are we *really* lost, Pooh?" Piglet asked, after they had gone this way a little bit . . .

. . . and then had turned around and had gone that way a little bit, and had not found Eeyore or the path they had left.

Pooh sat down on a log and Piglet sat down with him. "If somebody would just find us, we wouldn't be lost at all," Pooh explained to Piglet. "I do wonder where they all are."

Piglet sighed. "What should we do, Pooh?"

"Let's talk very loud, and interestingly, and maybe someone will come close to hear what we're saying," Pooh suggested.

So they talked using loud words, and soon they decided the best loud words were names.

"Christopher Robin!"
"Eeyore!"
"Owl!"
"Rabbit!"

Things to remember so you don't get lost:
Stay on the trail.
Always have someone with you.
Take a whistle with you.
If you are lost, stay in one place and blow!

Pooh and Piglet suddenly heard a tiny voice. "You were talking in such big voices that you woke me up," it said.

From under a pine cone by the log where Pooh and Piglet were sitting the owner of the tiny voice looked at them sleepily and yawned.

"Why, it's Very Small Beetle," said Pooh to Piglet.

"You're lost, you know," Piglet told him.

"Rabbit has everyone looking for you," Pooh said.

"Then let's go find him," said Very Small Beetle, and he led Pooh and Piglet back to the path where Eeyore was waiting.

While they were "lost," Pooh and Piglet added to their collections.
Here are some of the things they found:

Pooh

moss

milkweed pod

twigs

rock with lichens

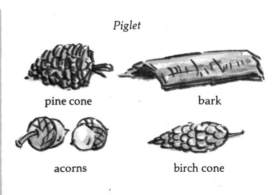

Piglet

pine cone

bark

acorns

birch cone

Pooh greeted Eeyore. "Look who we found," he said.

Very Small Beetle nodded politely to Eeyore.

"It's been very lonely here," Eeyore said sadly. "But then I'm always being left alone and kept waiting while others do interesting things." He looked at Very Small Beetle. "Where did you find him?"

"Well," squeaked Piglet, "we didn't exactly find him."

Pooh cleared his throat. "You might say that in his small way, he found us."

Here are some other *small* things to look for on a nature walk:

violet

different kinds of seeds

caterpillar

mushrooms (Just look—don't touch. Some are poisonous.)

snail

cocoon

It was Eeyore who started them moving again. "We should join Rabbit and the others and tell them we found Very Small Beetle," he said.

Piglet suggested that Very Small Beetle ride on Eeyore's back, which he did. And Pooh walked alongside, nibbling a bit of honey cake, which he had saved from lunch, to renew his strength.

They walked down the path towards Kanga's house.

On the way to Kanga's house, Very Small Beetle from his high perch on Eeyore's back pointed out some birds' nests to them.

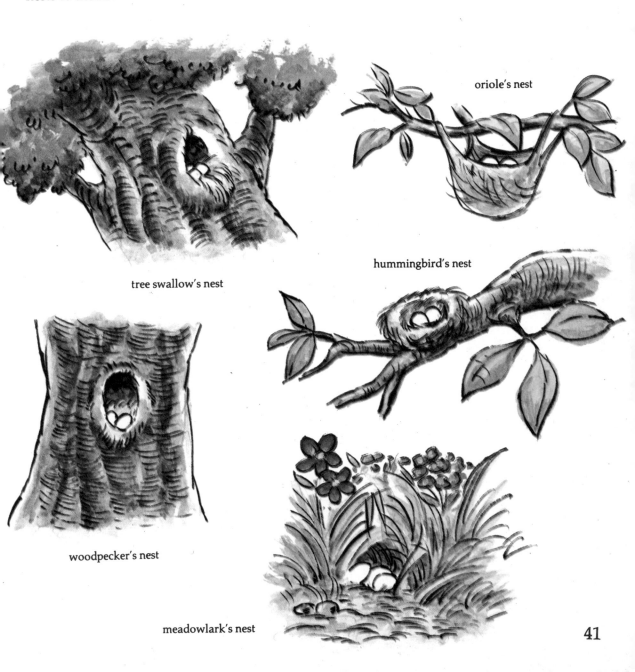

oriole's nest

tree swallow's nest

hummingbird's nest

woodpecker's nest

meadowlark's nest

41

The way to Kanga's house led across the stream and into the meadow where many of Rabbit's friends-and-relations lived.

Very Small Beetle tapped gently on Eeyore's ear. "If you don't mind, please let me off here," he requested. "This is home. Relatives, friends, and neighbors live here. You can tell Rabbit I wasn't lost at all. Just taking a long nap."

"Will there be a reward for finding you?" Eeyore asked.

"I doubt it very much," answered Very Small Beetle, as he scurried home.

"Wouldn't you know," said Eeyore.

Very Small Beetle wants you to meet some of his relatives:

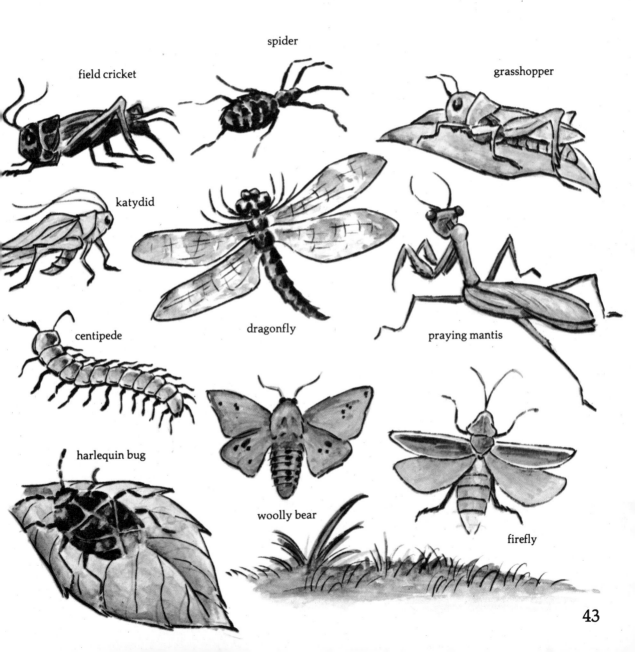

spider

field cricket

grasshopper

katydid

dragonfly

praying mantis

centipede

harlequin bug

woolly bear

firefly

43

When they reached Kanga's house everyone was glad to see everybody.

Rabbit was happy to hear that Very Small Beetle was safe and sound.

Eeyore and Owl were told how helpful they both had been.

Kanga and Roo wanted to see everything that Pooh and Piglet had collected, but Christopher Robin said, "Wait! I have a better idea."

He took both of the collecting bags. "Don't anyone leave," he said. "Owl, you can come with me."

"Left out again," Eeyore said. "Wouldn't you know."

They waited.

Before too long, Owl came back. "Everyone is invited to Christopher Robin's," he announced. "For a surprise."

Owl led the way to Christopher Robin's house. Everyone came, including Tigger and Very Small Beetle and lots of Rabbit's friends-and-relations.

When they came in sight of the house they saw a large sign which read:

THE HUNDRED ACRE WOOD NATURE SHOW

Christopher Robin had taken some of the things that Pooh and Piglet had found and put them on display. There were leaves and flowers, acorns and grasses, feathers and twigs, and many more interesting things to admire. It was a wonderful show, and Pooh and Piglet were both declared winners in the collecting contest.

THE HUNDRED-ACRE WOOD NATURE SHOW

After the show was over, Christopher Robin suggested that Pooh and Piglet stay and have a little snack.

"Like honey and butter sandwiches," suggested Pooh.

Christopher Robin nodded.

So they sat under a tree and snacked and talked about what a beautiful and busy day it had been.

"It was very clever of us," said Pooh finally, "to think of taking a nature walk."

And Piglet and Christopher Robin agreed.

SIR BRIAN'S CASTLE

RABBIT'S HOUSE

POOH'S HOUSE

SIX PINE TREES

PIGLET'S HOUSE

KANGA'S HOUSE

SAND PIT